Abuelita and I Make Flan

Adriana Hernández Bergstrom

Charlesbridge

Today is going to be amazing.

Plan for today

Make the *BEST* flan for Abuelo's birthday

Abuelita

Abuelo

Mami

Teo

↑ flan

Me (Anita) ←

I've never *actually* made flan before, but I know it will be great. . . .

Abuelita usually makes the flan.
She promised to teach me today.

Abuelita always flips the flan onto this plate.
It is from Cuba, and she's had it since forever
before I was born.

Today is Abuelo's birthday,
and I've already ruined it.

Maybe no one will notice?

Abuelita has arthritis. It makes it hard for her fingers to close all the way.

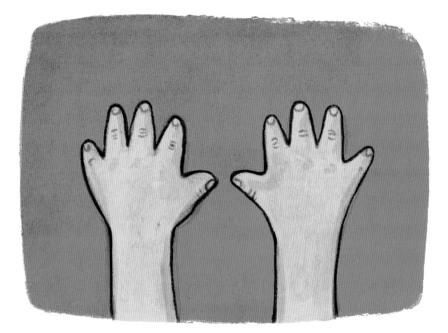

My hands are strong, and I'm her best helper. Usually.

threading
a needle

weeding

picking saffron
for rice

cutting coupons

opening jars

undoing knots

securing
necklaces

helping
with laundry

washing
the dog

Abuelita reads the recipe aloud.

eggs

memo

Flan de Queso

3/4 taza de azúcar
5 huevos
1 lata de leche condensada (dulce)
1 lata de leche evaporada
1 cucharita de vainilla
1 queso crema

SUGAR

I find the ingredients like
a scavenger hunt!
See, I *can* be
a good helper.

sugar
(Ants can't open
the fridge.)

cream
cheese

evaporated milk

sweetened
condensed milk

baking
mold

pan

A flan needs lots of eggs.
Abuelita teaches me how to crack them.

Your tía abuela Marta had a recipe for a party flan that used twenty-five yemas and two pounds of sugar!

She taught me to crack eggs like this . . . con cuidado.

Flan cooks in a water bath to help it
bake evenly.
I turn on the water to fill the pan.

I pour the sugar, and Abuelita makes the caramel.

We pour the mix into the mold.

Together we close the oven door
and do a little dance.

Together we wait.

And wait.

And wait.

Did I ever tell you the story of the plato de cristal? Tu bisabuela Catalina bought it for our five-year aniversario after your abuelo . . .
Do we really need to tell that story on my birthday?
TTTTTTTTTTT

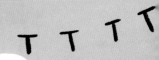

Aghh! The flan is almost done.

We need Abuelita's special plate, but it's in a million pieces!

I can't keep this secret any longer....

I am sorry, Abuelita. I was so excited to make flan that I went to see the super special plato de cristal you always use from Cuba from bisabuela Catalina but when I went to see it, my chancleta slipped and I lost my balance, and I grabbed the doile and everything came down and the plato broke. I didn't know how to fix it for Abuelo's birthday. I hope you still love me. I know it was special.

Abuelita sets the flan to cool.

About that plato: Abuelo broke the original taking it out of the box at our wedding in front of everyone! This one was a replacement.

¡Qué pena! All in front of tu mamá. She had just given it to us!

I have a new plan!

Abuelita takes my special plate.
I hope it works.

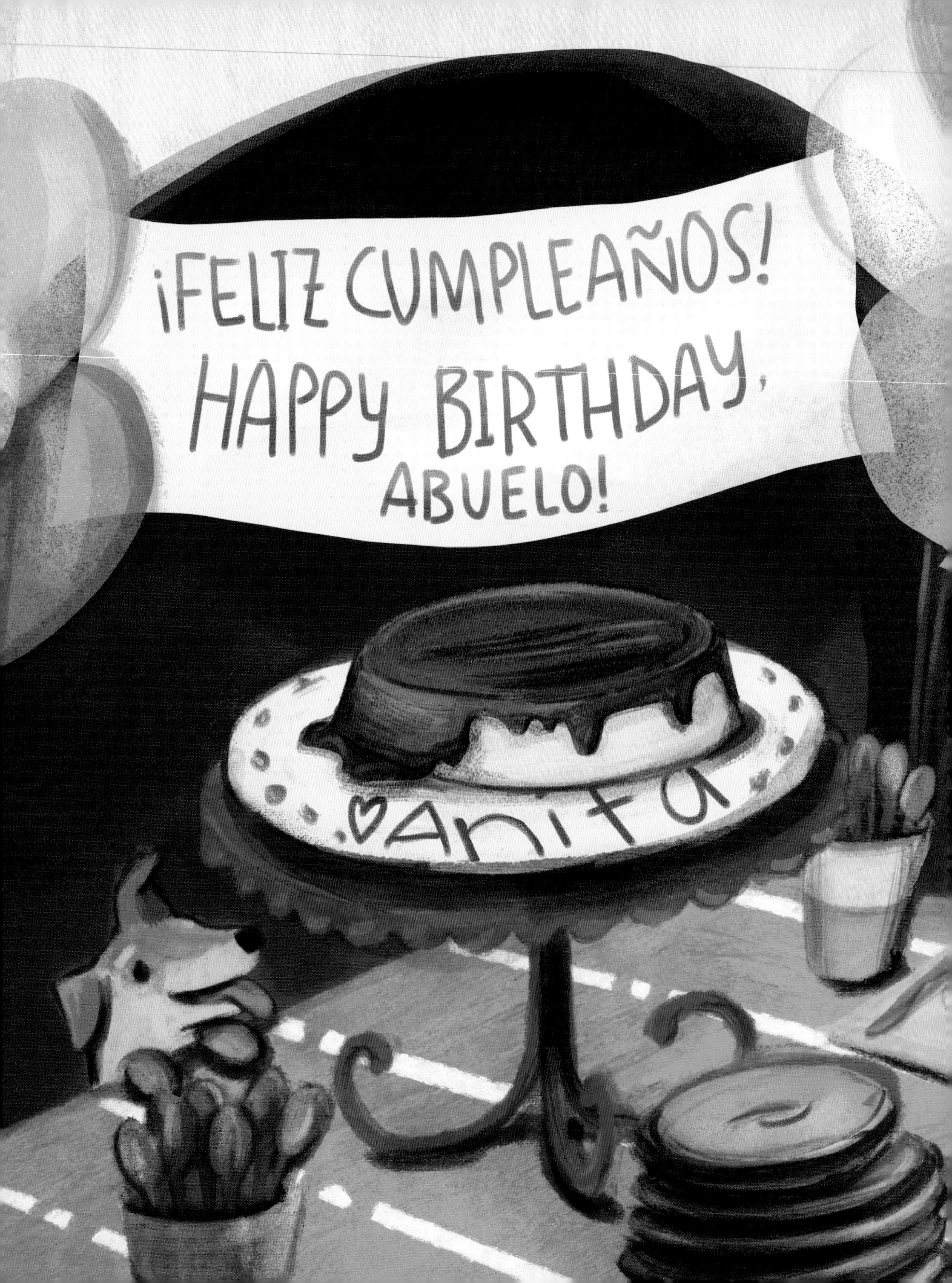
¡FELIZ CUMPLEAÑOS!
HAPPY BIRTHDAY,
ABUELO!
Anita

We make a great team!

Recipe for Cheese Flan

Ingredients

3/4 cup granulated sugar
5 eggs
1 [14 oz] can evaporated milk
1 [12 fl oz] can sweetened
   condensed milk
1 teaspoon vanilla
1 [8 oz] package cream
   cheese, softened

Tools

1 round 9" circular baking mold
1 bain-marie (an oven-safe
   pan large enough to hold
   the flan's baking pan and
   water; also called a water
   bath)

Instructions

Please get adult assistance and supervision when cooking
with a hot stove.

1. Preheat oven to 350°F (175°C).

2. Have an adult make the caramel: Heat the sugar in a pan,
   stirring frequently, until it turns amber. Pour the caramel in
   the baking mold, rotating to coat the bottom evenly.

3. In a blender, add the eggs, evaporated milk, sweetened
   condensed milk, and vanilla. Add the cream cheese in pieces.
   Blend until smooth. Pour into the baking mold and cover
   with foil.

4. Prep the bain-marie by filling it with 1 inch of water, and place
   it in the oven. Next, place the baking mold (foil side up) into the
   water bath. Bake for 45 minutes to 1 hour or until the batter is
   jiggly, not runny.

5. Remove from the oven and let rest for 25 minutes. Chill in
   the fridge for at least 3 hours or overnight. Flip the flan by
   removing the foil, running a knife along the edge of the mold,
   and inverting the mold onto a bigger serving dish. Spoon the
   remaining caramel sauce from the mold onto the flan.
   Serve and enjoy!

Translations

(in order of appearance)

flan—caramel custard dessert

abuelo—grandfather

abuelita—granny

sí—yes

mi niña—my girl

paciencia—patience

taza de azúcar—cup of sugar

huevos—eggs

lata de leche condensada (dulce)—can of sweetened condensed milk

lata de leche evaporada—can of evaporated milk

cucharita de vainilla—teaspoon of vanilla

queso crema—cream cheese

tía abuela—great aunt

yemas—egg yolks

con cuidado—carefully

despacito—slowly

para que no me salpique—so it won't splatter me

tu bisabuela—your great-grandmother

hacía un flan de coco de lo más delicioso—used to make a really delicious coconut flan

plato de cristal— crystal plate

aniversario—anniversary

ven conmigo—come with me

mira—look

Es posible.—Possibly yes.

mamá—mother

¿Qué pasa?—What's the matter?

mijita—contraction of mi + hijita, literally means "my daughter," but used as a general term of endearment and pronounced like "mee-HEE-tah"

chancleta—sandal, slipper

doile—doily

mi cielo—my sky

¡Qué pena!—How embarrassing!

¡Buena idea!—Good idea!

uno, dos, y . . . —one, two, and . . .

¡Feliz cumpleaños!—Happy birthday!

perfecto—perfect

My abuelo (center) in his judogi, Havana, Cuba, 1957

My abuelita (left) and tía abuela Marta (center), and me in Miami, 1988

This book is dedicated to my abuelita Kukí, abuela Kuka, tía abuela Marta, Abuelito, and the Cuban diasporic village-and-a-half that raised me. Thank you. I miss you.—A. H. B.

Published by Charlesbridge
9 Galen Street
Watertown, MA 02472
(617) 926-0329
www.charlesbridge.com

Printed in China
(hc) 10 9 8 7 6 5 4 3 2 1

Library of Congress Cataloging-in-Publication Data
Names: Hernández Bergstom, Adriana, author, illustrator.
Title: Abuelita and I make flan / by Adriana Hernandez Bergstrom; illustrated by Adriana Hernandez Bergstrom.
Description: Watertown, MA: Charlesbridge Publishing, [2022] | Audience: Ages 5–8. | In English with some Spanish words. | Summary: Anita helps her grandmother make flan for her grandfather's birthday.
Identifiers: LCCN 2021017084 (print) | LCCN 2021017085 (ebook) | ISBN 9781623542658 (hardcover) | ISBN 9781632898890 (ebook)
Subjects: LCSH: Grandparent and child—Juvenile fiction. | Grandmothers—Juvenile fiction. | Cooking—Juvenile fiction. | Desserts—Juvenile fiction. | CYAC: Grandmothers—Fiction. | Cooking—Fiction. | Desserts—Fiction. | Cuban Americans—Fiction.
Classification: LCC PZ7.1.H49454 Ab 2022 (print) | LCC PZ7.1.H49454 (ebook) | DDC [E] —dc23
LC record available at https://lccn.loc.gov/2021017084
LC ebook record available at https://lccn.loc.gov/2021017085

Display type set in Clochard by Hanoded
Text type set in Grenadine by Mark van Bronkhorst and Family Dog Fat by Jakob Fischer
Color separations and printing by 1010 Printing International Limited in Huizhou, Guangdong, China
Production supervision by Mira Kennedy
Designed by Jon Simeon